THE
REALM
TRAVELER

BETHANY BELLEMIN

Copyright © 2024 Bethany Bellemin.

All rights reserved. No part of this book may be reproduced, stored, or transmitted by any means—whether auditory, graphic, mechanical, or electronic—without written permission of both publisher and author, except in the case of brief excerpts used in critical articles and reviews. Unauthorized reproduction of any part of this work is illegal and is punishable by law.

ISBN: 979-8-89419-127-0 (sc)
ISBN: 979-8-89419-128-7 (hc)
ISBN: 979-8-89419-129-4 (e)

Because of the dynamic nature of the Internet, any web addresses or links contained in this book may have changed since publication and may no longer be valid. The views expressed in this work are solely those of the author and do not necessarily reflect the views of the publisher, and the publisher hereby disclaims any responsibility for them.

One Galleria Blvd., Suite 1900, Metairie, LA 70001
(504) 702-6708

To Victoria, Emily, Zebulun, Isaac, and Samuel:
You are all warriors, and I'm so honored to
face the battlefields of life beside you.

Part 1

Rynan stood nervously watching the murmuring court of the Forest Kingdom. The crowd moved and weaved about with their whispering like a horde of ants. Only the king was silent, standing in front of his throne, staring down at Rynan, the warrior who had failed in his service. Rynan had failed most shockingly; he admitted it to himself and to the court. He had left his post of guarding the magic wolf bane pup that would grow to be the next warrior beast of the kingdom. Each bane had been carefully guarded for many thousands of generations, and so long as one of their kind was in the king's service, the gremlins had never dared to attack the kingdom; but Rynan had stepped away for only a moment—at the time it seemed so small a thing. He had been lured by the soft music of a stranger playing the lute. Of course, now everyone realized the stranger had been a decoy to distract the guardian while the young wolf was taken away—and most likely taken to the Mount of the Dark Moon where the poor young one would be slain or imprisoned until the dusk of time. Rescue seemed impossible, for none who had ever dared to venture within the shadow of the mountain ever returned, and now the kingdom was an open target for the gremlins without magic to protect them.

The people were distressed and rightfully angry with the guardian for letting them be put in such danger, and here they all were gathered to see the punishment that Rynan would receive and to find out how the king could protect them now.

Finally, the king held up his hand, and silence pervaded the great hall. "Approach, Rynan, guardian of the magic bane."

Rynan slunk forward, his head down and eyes upon the marble floor.

"You have cost this kingdom much, perhaps our very existence. The last wolf bane is gone, and the gremlins will come. It will be a long time before the portals open to send another bane to our aid. You know more than anyone it can only happen once a generation. Our generation already received their bane, but now the magic is gone, and any wards the young pup had learned to wield will fail without his presence to enforce them. The next bane cannot be sent unless the wolf with us summons his successor, which cannot be done now that he is gone. The enemy will come now. Ancient scrolls tell us that in times past, only one other thing could protect us from the coming darkness."

Fear coursed through Rynan's veins, for he well knew what that one thing was.

The king's voice boomed in the echoing hall. "A drop of dragon's blood taken from the head of the dragon of the golden crest, from between his very eyes, and yet you know the dragon must not die in the shedding of his blood. That one drop must be brought to the pedestal in the room of prophecies and there kept until the generation is fulfilled and the next bane descends. On the final day of the allotted time, if unity has prevailed in the kingdom, the drop will turn to a golden sphere, illuminating with the light that shines into the stars, and it will bring a new wolf protector to our lands. During those years, there will be wars against the gremlins, for they will come to overrun us, but the drop of dragon's blood must be kept safe until the time expires. Unless this deed is done, we will surely perish without a hope."

There was such a silence as the hall had never witnessed.

"You know what you must do," the king said sternly.

Rynan nodded slowly. "I must retrieve the drop of dragon's blood and keep it safely on the pedestal for this generation's time."

The sentence was only more appalling because of the hopelessness of it. It was unlikely he would even survive the journey through the three realms, much less survive the encounter with the dragon, but Rynan wasted no time in despair, and he knew his history too well to doubt he deserved all the blame.

In ancient times, a chief had found a mage that could promise a way to defend against the constant attacks from the gremlins. The mage had unlocked a spell that brought a magic-wielding wolf, a being from the constellations. They were the ones that lived beyond the stars and possessed a powerful magic. The wolf came down to the Forest Kingdom and aligned himself with the stricken people. The wolf was a giant of a beast and, using magic and strength, had routed the evil. Since that day, when a wolf resigned his place, a young pup appeared as the next bane to watch over the kingdom. Each pup had to be protected until adulthood, and a human was always with it as caretaker for the rest of its life. This time of protecting kept a balance in the magic so the kingdom would not abuse the power residing with them. The guardian would not let the people use up the sacred magic for their own means, and the guardian also made sure the wolf had protection for when it enforced the wards or fought on the kingdom's behalf. There had been many wars over the centuries, but the power of each wolf always ensured victory. The ancient chief had been crowned the first king of the Forest Kingdom, and Rynan's ancestor had been assigned to watch over the first magic bane, the first guardian. Now Rynan had failed his entire lineage as well as his kingdom. He bowed deeply to the king and left the great hall, never once looking up.

Once outside the castle, he found his friend, Galsavia, a unicorn with a ruby set between his nostrils, waiting for him.

Rynan stopped in front of his friend, meeting his eye with grim determination. "My sentence is decided. I will fulfill the required law. I leave for the lands of the dragon of the golden crest."

"I will come," the unicorn said in that soft voice which they speak with when sad.

"You must not," Rynan began, but he did not finish.

"As surely as my name is Galsavia, I will not leave you, my friend. This is a duty where I can accompany you, and I will."

"Then so be it," Rynan responded gratefully.

The rest of the evening they used to pack two small satchels and study maps with the thoroughness of warring generals.

The next morning, while the moon still shone in the velvet sky, they set off beyond the borders of the Forest Kingdom into the unknown. The guards at the gate would not even give them a nod as they left. A courtier stood solemnly, holding the portal spear, a magic-made weapon that opened the doorway to leave the kingdom. The spear could not be used for fighting but was so full of power it sparked blue in the early morning light. Rynan accepted the heavy spear, and the courtier turned away without speaking.

The key to portal walking was heavy and awkward to carry, but they would make do. Armed with his sword, dagger, the portal key, and Galsavia's horn, they had only themselves to rely on. Rynan's heart was in his toes as he stepped out of the gate. He had never been outside of his kingdom. If Galsavia had not walked beside him, he wasn't sure he would have been able to take that first step to redeeming himself. Before them hung the portal, simmering with surges of power like lightning bolts. Rynan had never traveled through it; he took a deep breath. There was no going back. He had to make this right. Stepping through the portal brought a prickling sensation like electricity. As they emerged on the other side, a quiet stretch of beach awaited them—their first realm to traverse.

Far into the wide they traveled, to the waterfalls of the Siren on the far edge of her world. Rynan knew this first encounter would greatly determine his success for his mission; he needed something only the Siren could give—for as everyone knows the blood of a dragon will burn a hole through anything except a diamond vial made at the base of the Siren's waterfalls—but Rynan knew he could not receive a vial without giving something in return, and he was anxious about what the Siren would require.

The ancient texts had been very vague on this part of the exchange. He had studied the old lore faithfully in his many years as guardian, partially to possess all known knowledge to protect the magic bane but partly because his sense of duty was ingrained so deep all lore that could in any way affect the safety of his kingdom he needed to read and memorize. Who knew when that knowledge would prove useful. Today he was grateful for his bookish hobby though despite his sense of duty, he had still morbidly failed *in* doing his duty. He gritted his teeth from the physical pain his failure caused him. Beside him, Galsavia, sensing his turmoil, nudged his shoulder gently with his soft muzzle.

Rynan smiled over at his best friend. "I could not have the courage to do this quest without you."

Galsavia gave a short nod. Unicorns are well known to be mostly silent though very loyal companions.

They traveled for many days with the distant sea on their left and a wall of sand dunes on their right. It was a very silent and barren land. Only an occasional seagull added to the distant murmur of waves. Every evening they took turns guarding, for though it was only the very edge of the Forest Kingdom lands, there were still many dangers lurking in the stillness. They had barely enough food to survive the journey, and each day tolled by with no way to supplement their provisions. They didn't dare to stray to the ocean; the Siren would not accept them if she could smell they had eaten her fish. Even Galsavia struggled to find food, reduced to eating small prickly bushes that grew sparsely as they traveled. They were grateful for the frequent rainfalls as they would have died of thirst long before reaching their destination. The portal spear seemed to grow heavier every day, and Rynan used it as a staff, hoping that was not disrespectful to its power. Their next portal opening lay beyond the waterfalls of the Siren.

They reached the waterfalls on an evening, one month after they had begun their journey. A narrow path led down to the water's edge, and they walked it single file, walls of thorn bushes lining the way, making them leery to walk side by side. When they reached the falls, a cool mist washed over them; but no matter how much the water gurgled down the mountainside, the pool remained motionless like a mirror. Colors of blue, green, and silver glistened all around them.

"So…guests have come," a woman's voice spoke out, deep and mystical.

"Yes, my lady, we have traveled far," Rynan responded, for he knew that he must be respectful to her as he would his own queen. The Siren was easily angered.

"Rest here tonight. Tomorrow we will talk." Her voice echoed across the water then faded with the dusk.

They said no more, for the time was late, and they were careful to obey her laws. Rynan ate the last of his supplies, and Galsavia nibbled on the clover that grew upon the water's edge. Both were thirsty but would not dare to drink from the pool as the Siren had not given them permission to do so. As night covered the earth, they lay down back-to-back and slept. Far into the night, Rynan awoke with a start. An eerie and entrancing song wafted through fog and mist. He knew it was the Siren calling and that some ship upon a sea, if it obeyed her call, would come to its doom upon jagged, unforgiving rocks. He plugged his ears and thought hard on his duty, for he must not obey the call either. He must not fail again. He knew of many tales that some had tried to cross the water to her and had sunk beneath the motionless waters never to be seen again. Galsavia, being a unicorn, could not be bothered by her call, and he nuzzled against Rynan, encouraging him to be strong. The Siren's world was a death trap, and yet only she could craft the unbreakable diamond vials that could withstand the heat of the dragon blood.

At last, the agonizing night was at an end, and both travelers came to their feet. In the night, while she sang, the Siren had crafted three vials from the waterfalls mist, and they shimmered on the water's edge in the sunlight, blue and green and silver. As the sun shone upon the waterfall, the Siren stepped out from behind the curtain of water. She walked on legs—to his surprise; he had always thought the Siren would be a creature of water. Her dress was gray, and a knife was at her side. Her hair reached to her feet and shone blue and green and silver. She and her world were as one: living, breathing, deadly things. Her eyes were dark, and Rynan knew not to look into them, for her irises could drown you. He had heard of people losing themselves in her gaze, falling, gasping out their last breath to be forever separated from the earth. His mind was racing with the numerous studies of things he should know and remember for this meeting. At the moment, none of it seemed to be helping, merely adding fear to the intensity of the moment. The Siren was written about in many scrolls though he thought the writing did a poor job of actually preparing one to meet her.

Both friends bowed low, the unicorn's horn scraping against the ground.

She spoke, her speaking voice as deadly as her singing. "You have been honorable guests. You have not touched my waters, and now you may drink."

They did not need a second invitation; both quenched their thirst, and no water had ever tasted quite like the pool at the Siren's waterfalls.

When they had finished, Rynan bowed again. "We are honored to meet you."

She arched her eyebrow. "All say that when they arrive, but few say so when they leave...*if* they leave," she finished darkly. Rynan introduced himself and Galsavia.

She lifted her chin and stared, unblinking, at them. "I already know of you, guardian of the wolf bane. The sea spoke of you. It also told me you respected my fish. It is well for you that it is so."

Rynan decided to get to the point. "We have need of one of your vials, your ladyship."

She smiled a wan yet dangerous smile. "And what will you give in return for the vessel of priceless value?"

Rynan hesitated, for he knew he had nothing of great price. He had known a trade would be required though he rather hoped she would set him to complete a task instead of finding an item of value. He really could think of nothing that would interest the Siren. She had great wealth from the ships that crashed on her shores. She eyed him, her face judging his actions. He needed to find his voice. His hand brushed against the hilt of his sword, and he looked down. His sword was his father's. His father has been the guardian of the last magic bane, and in Rynan's heart, the weapon was priceless.

Slowly he drew it out and offered it to her, his head down. "It was my father's, and now, my ladyship, it is yours." He could not have known the meaning of what he offered, for no ancient writings told of this moment.

"You give me your sword?" she asked shrilly.

Rynan looked up and saw a terrifying look on her face.

"I demand your honor with it," she continued. She did not reach for his sword though she seemed to want it very badly indeed.

He nodded. "My honor goes with the weapon without asking." This calmed her somewhat.

"Long ago," she began. "I loved a common sailor and was willing to be mortal with him, but he had one last sailing to do. I crafted the first of my vials and placed my heart in it for him to keep in his travels, but the cursed man sold the heart from the sea for a king's ransom, but"—she laughed cruelly—"I sang my first song, and his ship crashed upon the rocks. He and his treasure lie forgotten in a watery grave, and so began my hatred of mankind. To do them ill, especially those upon the seas, is my greatest delight. The one thing I most desire is to have my heart back."

Rynan's own heart went to his toes. This was indeed a hopeless endeavor.

She saw his face and frowned. "You have promised your sword and your honor. Do you dare go back on your word? Are you a knight errant or merely a person of empty words?"

"It does not matter if I should dare, for once given, my word cannot go back" was his stout reply.

Her face smoothed. "Long ago, the king of the sea declared that a lost heart could be saved if one of noble honor wielded a sword to defend it, but it must be offered willingly." She gave Rynan a piercing look. He nodded back, his face calm. She continued. "At the bottom of this pool is the vial with my heart in it. I searched until I found it in the wreckage of my lover's ship and brought it back here, but alas, foolish I was to use the ancient magic on it! The magic placed upon rules that that no one except my lover can open the vial and release it. You must give up your heart to open that vial."

Rynan was silent. In a way, he ached her, for the Siren's life, one void of her heart and only filled with vengeance. He kept his tone neutral as he asked, "I must give my heart to you?"

"No, you fool! You must place it in the vial replacing mine—a heart for a heart. That is required in the magic of love."

"It is a dark love that takes so much," he replied quietly.

Her eyes shot sparks that hissed as they hit the water. *"How dare you!"* she thundered, raising her arm to strike him down, but he was quicker, and dodged behind a large boulder while her power crashed into the stone, shattering the veneer. Mortals could not withstand or deflect the destructive power of the Siren.

Rynan stood slowly, Galsavia watching him with concern and fear.

"May I ask a boon if I succeed?"

"What could you possibly wish for here at my pool?"

"I will retrieve the heart, but upon my returning it to you, you will give me all three vials to take with us on our journey."

"You ask too much!" she snarled.

"No, I ask out of need. Will you grant my request?"

She hesitated then gave a surly nod, and he stepped out from behind the rock. She handed him a necklace made from sea light, and he placed it around his neck.

"With that necklace, you may breathe and move freely in the water. Keep your sword with you. Do not fail like all the others…though I do not doubt that you will fail," she said coldly.

Rynan nodded and took off his heavy armor, laying it beside the portal spear. Then he said goodbye to Galsavia and dove into the pool. He found that he could move about and breathe quite like on land, as a large bubble of air created by the necklace cloaked him, and he easily found his way to the sandy bottom. He first saw a pile of skeletons, those who had failed before him. It was not an encouraging way to begin this venture.

The pool was very wide, and it took some time before he found the vial at last, half buried in the sand. He picked it up and saw the heart inside, beautiful and unmarred, like a perfect pearl.

If the Siren's words were true, his only course was to take out his own heart so that the vial would open. To release one, another must be imprisoned, and this seemed foolishness to him, so he did something else—something he believed would work, for he could not afford to fail. He had read in a long-forgotten scroll that a sealed heart could be freed by sincere love, but perhaps that did not mean it could not be the sincere love of friendship instead of romantic love, and the writings were very adamant that the love must not be false and must be proclaimed aloud. He held the vial up so that some of the sun's rays drifted down to it. But was his own heart sincere in this? Could he see the Siren as a friend?

"I release you!" he shouted at the top of his lungs.

The air cloaking him shuddered. A sound like a thunderbolt shook the pool, and the water moved for the first time in centuries. The dark magic, forged in anger and pain, that hoarded the Siren's heart did not want to give it up. Dark tendrils like smoky fingers grabbed his hands, trying to tear the vial away, but he held it with the strength of desperation as he was thrown about. His head struck a rock, and he knew he was bleeding, but still he held on. The magic began, trying to tear his necklace away, knowing then he would surely drown. With a great effort, he drew his sword and held it across his chest, pinning the necklace to him. In his left hand, he kept the vial up in the light. Was he truly willing to fight to the death for the Siren? He was willing to befriend her, but she would just as soon see him dead. Was she worth this danger? But he already knew the answer. He himself had made mistakes. He could not judge her for her own poor choices, but perhaps he could give her the hope to redeem herself.

"I release my friend! I will not yield!" He felt like his voice was being ripped from his throat. This time there was a great crack and the vial shattered in millions of stars and he realized the vial had reverted back to mist. The beautiful heart inside, still pure and untouched by anger or hate, shimmered brightly like a burnished jewel in his hand. Its glow permeated through the murkiness of the water and lit the darkness up as light as midday on land.

The magic was broken, the heart was free, and he had succeeded; but now the sea light in his necklace flared and winked out, his lungs burning as the water rushed into his air bubble. The weight of his sword dragged him down as he kicked desperately toward the murky ceiling that he hoped was the surface.

With a gasp, he floundered up into the light of late day. He was surprised as it had been morning when he first dove in. He had been in the battle for more than eight hours. Galsavia let out a loud neigh and charged through the water to him, his relief and joy overflowing.

Rynan hugged his friend's neck and let the unicorn pull him from the water. For a moment, he sagged on the sandy shore, catching his breath, then he turned to face the Siren. She was on her knees, and to his amazement, she was pale and shaking.

"You have succeeded and kept your heart. Can it be possible?" she asked, her voice choked with held-in sobs.

He smiled very kindly, understanding her better now. "It is possible, for you did not need a captive. You needed a friend," and he reached out, taking her hand and gently placing her heart there. She stared at it, her eyes slowly losing their fire; and when she at last looked up at him, he saw she was one of the merfolk. For on her forehead had appeared a crown of ocean crystals and seashells.

"How can you have succeeded though? How? You're so young and inexperienced."

Rynan laughed a little and gave a small smile. "Even a small fish can make big ripples."

She nodded, still staring at the glittering heart she held. "I was a mermaid queen until I loved a mortal then I came to land to join him, but after our relationship was ended, I could not return to the sea without a heart. Nothing in the sea is heartless. I had no place there with my hollow soul, but now I am restored because of you, guardian. I will be a maid of the sea again and will no longer live to destroy men." She smiled, a true smile this time, and asked, "Why the three vials, guardian? Why do you wish for all three?" She handed the perfect prism pieces to him.

Rynan accepted the priceless vials. "I will keep the treasures I find along the way in these vials, and when we return to our kingdom, perhaps they will help to heal the hurt I have caused my people."

"That's a precious thought, young warrior," she responded, and a tear fell, a mermaid tear, and Rynan caught it on the tip of his finger, for it was more precious than gold. He carefully poured it into one of the three vials. "The first of my found treasures," he said kindly.

Then she laughed, a pure ringing sound. Her face and hair continued to transform back to her original appearance. Her mermaid tail finally appeared, and she threw herself into the water. When she resurfaced, she had a large seashell. She handed it to him. "And here is a treasure you may keep as well. Fill this shell with water from the pool, and it shall sustain you when there is nothing else. It will not run dry until your quest is complete."

He bowed and accepted the gift, filling it with water from the shimmering pool. "Goodbye, my lady Siren," he said with another bow.

"Now I return to my former name, young warrior. I am no longer the Siren. They used to call me Thalassa. I shall take up that name again. Should you ever have need of help, send for me, and I will come."

With a wave, she dove into the waters, and he watched her sparkling form as she made her way back to the sea. As he watched, the surface on the pool began to ripple like ordinary water. The dark hue faded away to clear, and he could see to the bottom. The darkness was healed for the waterfalls of the Siren.

Once again Rynan and Galsavia took up their quest for the blood of the dragon. Rynan held out the spear before him and drove it into the ground. There was a shudder, and the portal bloomed out into the air before them. This time he was less hesitant and prepared the vibrating feel of the magic. The two friends stepped through to the next realm of their journey.

Part 11

Once entering the next realm, Rynan and Galsavia traveled as quickly as they could, their minds ever focused on the final land in the lair of the dragon of the golden crest. Rynan never ceased to think of the wolf's magic bane, lying in a dungeon deep in the heart of the mountain of the dark moon. He refused to think the pup was dead, and he knew he must make it right, but he did not know how. He only knew that once his quest was complete, somehow he would have to rescue the young creature. Often he thought back to the horrid moment where the lute player appeared, face cloaked in shadows. The player's instrument gleamed with starlight and trickled glitter as the strings were plucked. The song made his mind think of seas and stars, a place far away from his lands, where the pressure of being guardian could not follow him. His heart told him to ignore it, but his mind was dull and seemed to make him walk step after step as he followed the musician deep into the gardens away from the sleeping pup's cabin. Then behind him, he had heard the wolf pup cry out in fear. The musician gave a wicked laugh and had vanished while Rynan raced back to his post, sickened with fear to find the magic bane gone with no trace.

Thinking through these memories, Rynan berated his foolishness to himself and trudged on with more determination than before. They would succeed in their mission—they *had* to. If it had not been for the steady calmness of Galsavia, Rynan feared he would have lost his mind with only his morose thoughts to keep him company.

This realm proved to be a test of their perseverance, for this was the land of the giants. Every hill, every tree, every creature was abnormally large, and Rynan was less than pleased to notice the birds of prey here were nearly the size of dragons. This world was often called the uncharted lands, for giants did not record their world in writings and no humans dared to cross here—until now. It was unfortunate that this realm had to be crossed, but only two portals opened into the dragon's realm. One could be opened here in the land of the giants. The other was in the land of the spinners: the spiders' realm. Due to its highly venomous inhabitants, Rynan and Galsavia thought the giants would be the more likely to give them a chance of survival.

A great chasm ran alongside the ancient road they walked, splitting the realm in two. They were aware that at some point, it would need to be crossed. Rynan had been told by old lore that a massive bridge spanned the chasm: a bridge built by the hands of the first giant. It was the only place one could cross the great gulf. It seemed that such a large structure would be easy to find, but Rynan and Galsavia walked many miles and many days before he saw it upon the horizon. Reaching it at last, they were dismayed to see it in great disrepair. Massive stones and bricks that made up the structure had fallen away into the bottomless space below, and the gaps were very wide in between. As they hesitated at the foot of the bridge, a shadow passed over them. Both looked up to see a buzzard but ten times the size of any they had seen.

They looked at each other, then Rynan shrugged. "I doubt he's hovering around, waiting for us to die," but he did not feel as nonchalant as he sounded.

They then began to cautiously maneuver their way across the decrepit bridge, but eventually, they reached a hole along the opposite side that was beyond Rynan's abilities.

Galsavia whinnied and nodded to Rynan. "Here, my friend, you must ride."

"But it is too far for you to make it with me upon your back!" Rynan objected.

The unicorn shook his head. "If we fall, we fall, but there is no chance for you any other way."

And no more was said. Rynan swung upon the magnificent back, feeling very humbled at yet another sacrifice from his friend, for it is the greatest sacrifice of a unicorn to demean himself by being ridden. Galsavia snorted, flexed his powerful shoulders, and galloped straight at the hole, taking off as if he had wings. His leap was so powerful that it threw him across the hole and onto the ground across the chasm. Both rolled to their feet and laughed shakily. The ground was as a desert and barren as far as the eye could see, but they still laughed because for now, at least they had survived.

The laugh died in their throats when the ground suddenly trembled. Again and again, it shuddered beneath their feet. Rynan slowly turned about to see what he feared. A giant as tall as ten grown trees was walking toward them, his face as angry as a summer storm.

He stopped before them and bellowed, "You shrimp who dare to trespass in my lands! I shall feed you to my buzzard for supper!" And here, as if on cue, the buzzard circled in and landed on the shoulder of the giant.

Rynan held the spear firmly in his left hand and with his right drew his sword and saluted. "I am Rynan and have come with my friend Galsavia. We are traveling through your lands but will take nothing."

"You will take nothing certainly, for you shall be too dead to do harm, having dared to trespass here without paying tribute!" the giant thundered and reached toward them menacingly.

Galsavia drove his horn into the huge hand so that the giant bled, but the giant merely shook him off as if he were a hornet and grabbed them both up. Rynan slashed at the giant's face, but the giant squeezed him so tight in his fist that Rynan fainted and came to just as they entered the giant's castle. Over the doorway were three holes, as if it were missing three stones, and they were small perfect holes in the castle's face. Rynan's mind was functioning properly since blacking out, but he had the vague notion that he ought to know something about those empty holes.

Inside it was dark and dank and smelled of dead things from generations past. The giant threw them into separate cells before storming away and leaving them in a silence only broken by the dripping of slime that crept down the dungeon walls. Rynan wasted no time looking for way of escape. The giant had not even bothered to disarm him, deeming his sword and spear too insignificant to bother with. He could faintly hear Galsavia beating his hooves against the cell walls. Of course, Rynan tried to break the lock, but rusted as it was, it still held firm.

At last, worn out with exertion and hunger, he wrapped his cloak around him and rested. He checked the three vials not because he needed to but because it encouraged him. They glittered and cast a soft light about the cell, and he thought of far-off places and cool clear waters. At last, he fell asleep.

His dreams were not pleasant ones—he saw the wolf pup taken and the face of the stranger with the lute laughing malignantly before vanishing away without a trace. He dreamed that the gremlins had won a great war, and the Forest Kingdom was flooding until he could not breathe from drowning. He woke with a start to find his cell was full of water, lapping up to his nose. He leapt to his feet and waded to the cell door. A gutter at the end of the dungeon had water gushing out of it, and he realized that it must be storming in the outside world, and still the water came. He screamed for Galsavia to answer, but no voice responded.

At last, the water was so high his head slammed against the roof in his cell. He thought the end had surely come when he felt a huge hand grab him. The giant had come down just in time and pulled both of his prisoners out of the dungeon. Galsavia had been completely submerged and was nearly dead. The giant threw them down upon the hearth of his great fire, and Rynan was soon relieved to see the unicorn revive. For some time, the giant did not speak; he merely observed his prisoners, the giant buzzard keeping a cold eye on them from his perch in the rafters.

Finally, the giant thundered, "Have you any tribute to pay for your passage?"

Rynan hesitated then stood to his feet. He needed to strategize here. The only thing of value was the mermaid tear, but he was saving that for something of greater importance; the tear was not something he could afford to lose. He needed another plan. "I will pay service to you with any deed you require."

"Oh ho! You think you can do anything I cannot do myself? And this deed will be your payment to cross my lands?"

Rynan nodded.

The giant sneered, "Subdue my one enemy, and I shall let you free."

"Both of us shall go free?"

"Yes, the flesh of a unicorn is too salty for my taste."

"Who is this enemy?"

For answer, the giant carried him to a window and pointed. On the horizon, he could make out a cave with ornate carvings around the opening.

"There lies the gate of the cobra. The great snake lives there and slithers out often to devour my sheep. Destroy him, and you will be free."

Rynan looked at Galsavia and thought for a moment. The unicorn gave him a short nod, and Rynan answered "I will face him, but should I succeed, I may cross your paths anytime I wish and will not pay any tribute, and you will repair the bridge to make my journey easier."

The giant laughed loudly. "You make a great deal for one so small, but I doubt you will win. I do not believe I will have to honor your demands."

Rynan felt in his deepest heart that his failure was quite likely, but he stood as tall and held his head up. "Nevertheless, I will try."

The giant unbolted his door and motioned both of them forward.

"At least the cobra will be too full after eating you to bother my flocks today." Then he abruptly slammed the door.

Rynan felt ill as he looked ahead to the cave. He left the portal spear leaning against the giant's castle wall; it couldn't be used in a fight as its tip was only sharpened by magic when opening the gates. He knew giants could portal walk without the aid of magic items. No one would steal it here. He sighed heavily. Another task, another chance to disgrace himself, and this time the stakes were higher. Galsavia was with him, and if he failed, his friend could be hurt or worse.

"Why is it that in history, the heroes all seem so flawless and unflinching?" he murmured to himself.

Galsavia snorted beside him. "History is kinder than reality. The details of their life are hidden and lost behind the glory of their victories."

"Yes, but they are heroes for a reason."

"Because they got back up when they fell…and, Rynan, they definitely fell at times. No hero is perfect."

Rynan swallowed and took a deep breath. Perhaps his friend had a point, but at the moment, heroes of history did seem *very* much larger than life.

Galsavia looked at Rynan, "I think it's likely that many of them would have been afraid facing a giant snake."

Rynan shared a chuckle with the unicorn, then Galsavia said in a very serious tone, "If today does go against us and the snake should win, you must escape and survive. I will stay, and the serpent may feast on me. No, do not argue. You must survive to finish the mission."

Rynan clenched his jaw in determination, or else he thought he might let his nerves get the best of him, and they went onward with that cloud hanging over them.

When they reached the cave of the cobra, they stopped. The carvings so elaborate at a distance proved to be distorted fangs and the face of a snake, and they had to walk into its stone mouth to enter the cave. It unnerved them badly and nearly robbed them of the last ounce of courage they possessed, but they continued into the mouth of the cave, sword drawn and horn poised for action.

Rynan hung the vials on his belt as a light to see by as they walked deeper and deeper into the darkness. The scuff of his boots against sand and rock seemed horribly loud in the silence. For some time, the way was pitch black, then he thought he saw a faint glowing.

At first, he thought he was imagining things, for it looked like faint stars glittering on the ceilings and walls of the cave. Then he realized that there were thousands of stones, in many colors, glowing like fire and water. It was stunning to behold, and it finally dawned on Rynan that he was in the cave of elements. History told of stones of priceless value that possessed the power of wind and rain and fire, and these stones were coveted by kings to keep their kingdom prosperous, for crops grew and lands flourished wherever these stones were held.

Long ago the location of these stones was lost to the world. The miners had vanished without a trace, and only they knew where to find the powerful rocks. Now Rynan knew he had an answer that had been lost for a thousand years. Most people had doubted if the tale was even true. It seemed to Rynan that the snake must have come long ago and eaten the workers; with their demise, the location of the wonderful stones had been lost. These thoughts raced through his mind as they continued deeper into the interior.

Rynan felt rather than saw the snake. A large, slimy presence began to pervade his senses, and Galsavia's nostrils flared wide.

"Sooooo, I have companyyyyy." A silky slippery voice spoke out of the blackness. "Two of you, I ssssee…but will you leave herrrre?"

Rynan held his sword out and answered, "Two have come, and two will leave."

"You think you can change what otherssss could not? You think you can rid the world of the demon that isssss me? I'm ssssure the giants laugh at your impossssssible optimism."

Rynan gritted his teeth. He would not let the creature of nightmares sway him—not now, not ever. Too much was at stake. "Others may scoff, but that does not stop my determination. Those who would change the world are hated by those who are complacent. Nothing changes if everyone is apathetic."

"Ssss-sssss. Brave sssspeaker, but you will tasssste like all the othersss," and with a shivering hiss, the cobra lunged at him, mouth gaping open, venom dripping from its fangs.

Rynan and Galsavia dove separate ways to avoid the enemy as they had done before in battles. It was not surprising that the snake chose to follow Rynan. Rynan ran and put his back to the wall of the cave, for he did not want the serpent to be able to get behind him with his long body. The snake wove and weaved about, striking and hissing, while Rynan was dodging and stabbing. It was a losing battle. The venom was dripping all over him, causing his skin to burn and making it hard to breathe, but still he fought. He knew that Galsavia's horn stabbed the reptile many times because brown blood was flowing freely from the long body. Rynan's blade stung true many times also, and yet it did not seem to bother the beast in any way. Both guardian and unicorn felt an exhaustion and sickness as they never had before, and it looked as if the battle would end soon and the ending would not go well for them. Rynan was blocking a long fang back with his sword when an idea occurred to him.

"Galsavia, watch the tail. I will watch fangs!" he cried out as he dodged another strike.

Galsavia responded, jumping in and stabbing at the tail that was whipping toward Rynan's head.

Gasping for breath, Rynan sang out, "Foolish beast that never conceded defeat before, you shall never eat again!"

Then he abruptly stepped back, withdrawing his sword and snatching his dagger back. The snake devoured him in one bite. As he felt the muscles push him down the throat, he struck his dagger out with his left hand and his sword with his right. Using both blades, he raked them down the throat of the creature. The snake screamed, shuddered, and collapsed, its body writhing grotesquely in its demise. Rynan climbed out of the large gash he had made, dripping with venom, but relatively unharmed.

Galsavia galloped over and let Rynan lean against him. With the small ounce of energy he had left, Rynan broke a venom-filled fang off the gaping snake's mouth as proof of the victory to show the giant. He also stopped and chipped several of the element stones from the wall. He took some fire stones, some of the rain stones, and some wind. The fire stones glowed red and shimmered as if a real fire was concealed within. The rain stones glowed blue and rippled as if containing water, and the wind stones were a pale white and vibrated in his hand like a powerful breeze coursed inside it. Each stone was a perfect circle.

He placed one of each of these stones within the second Siren's vial and filled his pockets with the others. Then the two friends slowly made their way back to the castle.

The giant opened his door at their knock and nearly fell down in amazement. "You escaped the serpent's lair?" he boomed.

Rynan's answer was raising the fang up.

"Can it be so...the serpent is dead?" the giant said incredulously as he stared at the fang.

"Dead as dead can be," Rynan murmured, his knees shaking so that he could barely stand.

"I suppose you want the bargain fulfilled," the giant barked, his face growing angry at the thought.

Rynan aimed the fang at the giant's foot. "Fulfill it, or I will give you a dose of cobra. It would be most unpleasant."

Now above all, giants respect bravado especially when it's an act of daring desperation, and this giant was duly impressed—so impressed that he did something very unexpected.

"I suppose I must need to keep my word. Please come in and be my guest tonight," and he swept them into the castle without more ado. Giants do not entertain guests and loathe all forms of company, but this giant was true to his word though a bit surly about all of it, for as anyone knows, a giant is happiest when he is grouchy. That night both friends slept well in large comfortable beds and woke late the next day.

After waking, the giant fed them a feast and packed fresh provisions for their journey. Before they left, the giant brought out a human-sized sword which he presented to Rynan. It was a two-edged blade with strange writings on the hilt and a carving of an oak tree.

"Show this to any giant, and you may walk freely among us at any time. It belonged to a warrior from long ago, his name is lost to history, but I do know that the tales say when he wielded this sword, no enemy could withstand his power. He left the weapon with my grandfather and said to give it to the one that would follow after him."

Rynan bowed as he accepted the gift, and the giant bowed back. "How do you know I'm the one worthy to have this sword?"

The giant gave a rare smile. "Do you see any other warriors lining up to face serpents and walk fearlessly through the land of strangers to fulfill his mission? There have been none like you until now."

Rynan looked down at the gift, humbled and curious about this past warrior. Turning back to the moment at hand, he reached into his pocket. "And I also have a gift for you, great one." Then Rynan presented three stones—one rain, one wind, and one fire. "Place these above your doorway. I warrant they will fit there, for once long ago I believe that stones such as these graced your castle entrance."

The surprised giant did as he was bid, placing the stones in the marked place, and instantly the harsh hot wind died down to a pleasant spring breeze. Grass began to grow beneath their feet, and a vine sprouted up the side of the castle with flowers bursting into bloom before their very eyes.

"The land is healed!" the giant said hoarsely, and he turned incredulous eyes to Rynan.

"As in the days of old, when the giants were a dwelling in a land of beauty," the warrior replied.

"In truth, I did not think these days could return to this land."

"Now you have those days again. Guard them well."

The giant nodded and gazed about. "I will," he replied firmly. Then he turned back to Rynan. "Travel well, my little friend. I will have the bridge repaired by your return according to my bargain, and should you need help, call for me by my name, Jahonbran. I should be glad to do a good turn to the one who slew the cobra and brought beauty back to my eyes"

A giant is honorable, if he is nothing else, and he sent the two away with lasting friendship and again repeating the promise to come to their aid should they ever need it. A long gray rope was in the supplies—a rope braided by a giant and would never break or fray—a gift of immeasurable value.

Rynan and Galsavia went forward on the journey with their hearts lighter and courage renewed, and Rynan with the vials hanging at his side and two swords at his reach began to feel as if perhaps they would succeed after all; perhaps there was a chance. The heavy spear weighed in his hand like an assurance, a promise that not all magic was angry with him for his failure.

Far ahead of them, they saw the mountains on the far side of the realm. Lingering like a haze was a shimmering light marking the place to open the portal.

Part III

Rynan and Galsavia traveled swiftly through the uncharted lands keeping the mountains in view. They encountered a few other giants along the way. One glance at Rynan's blade from Jahonbran, and they let him pass with a respectful nod. Because of the blade, they were able to travel quickly, which was good for Rynan, for each day he felt more and more the need to rescue the wolf pup if he could though he had yet to form a plan in his mind of how it might be possible. His dreams began to be more about the wolf calling for him, and he would awake with a jolt to see Galsavia watching him sympathetically.

After waking from one such nightmare, Rynan jerked to his feet, walking about in the cool night air, trying to calm his racing heart. After watching him for a few moments, Galsavia rolled to his feet and stepped in front of his pacing friend.

"We'll get him back." The soft voice of the unicorn brought a small surge of peace to Rynan's soul, but his mind could not relax.

Rynan nodded absently. His friend believed in him though he felt that level of trust might be misplaced considering how they had ended up here. They had many obstacles to encounter before the chance to save the pup.

Galsavia must have known his thoughts, for he continued speaking. "I will be by your side until we succeed in our journey, and when this is over, I will be by your side while you save the magic bane. But first, Rynan, you have to save yourself."

Rynan glanced at the unicorn, confused at the words and surprised his friend was talking so much; long conversations are rare for unicorns. "What do you mean by that?"

"Your guilt has trapped you. You cannot hope to succeed in freeing the wolf from his physical cage until you are no longer trapped in your mental cage."

"I have to save him and the world from my mistakes. I deserve my guilt."

"No, my friend." Galsavia spoke with surprising force. "You have to help them save themselves. You alone cannot save the world. Everyone has to realize they need saving and rise up to fight. A war cannot be won with only one soldier. Do not let guilt be a disease that holds you down. Rather, let it be the tool that sharpens your weapons. The world is a big place to believe it all rests on you, my friend, and you are not alone, Rynan, guardian of the magic bane. You have been lonely, yes, but you've never been alone."

Rynan thought back through his life. Being guardian was a strict, isolated role. The endless rules could be suffocating: to always be held on a pedestal, to remain untouched by worldly times, to always remain solely focused on the wolf in your charge, to always be above reproach in your duties and actions, to be respected, but always be diligent to deserve that respect.

Rynan had felt alone and overwhelmed, but Galsavia had always been there, not so much physically by his side but in spirit. The brief greetings when seeing each other go about their work, the kind smiles and nods of acknowledgment, the eye contact alone had been comforting. Galsavia had reached out as far as their positions allowed and touched the heart of the lonely boy that was growing into a man with the weight of the world on his shoulders—a man that lived his life in fear of failure until the day he did actually fail. Having let his guard down for a moment had cost him losing a lifetime of work in the process while endangering the one who depended on him most.

The song that had lured him away, entranced with the spell of deception, was never as loud as the hammering guilt in his head. His moment of failure had cost him everything he knew, and yet when all others turned away from him, Galsavia had been there. When others refused to offer any help in his assignment to undo his wrong, Galsavia had come. Rynan didn't feel he deserved this dedication or loyalty. He hung his head, and the unicorn stepped in, draping his neck over Rynan's shoulder. Rynan answered the hug, feeling like his heart would break with the relief that he was never alone and never would be. Someone believed in him.

No more words were spoken, and they left before sunrise to continue walking the path before them. At last, they came to the portal's passage site. Striking the spear into the ground, they saw the gate materialize, this one outlined in stones that seemed especially massive and ancient. As they passed through the gate into another world, all Rynan could think was how very warm it seemed in this portal until they exited to the other side, and he saw why. It was no wonder the dragon's realm was called the scorched lands. The land where dragons dwelt and practiced their art of fire spewing on trees and bushes left behind a blackened charred landscape devoid of all green things. Traveling here meant there would be no place to hide from threats. They were fully exposed to elements and predators.

In the far distance, a volcano glowed red against the pale sky, and the wind was unbearably hot. Rynan and Galsavia moved at a rapid pace in the direction of the massive volcano on the horizon. That was the abode of the dragon of the golden crest.

A few small dragons flew overhead and roared, but they only spit a few sparks. These smaller dragons were not interested in bothering an armed warrior with a look of battle on his face. A large murky river rushed and swirled along beside the path beside them, and in the distance, booming thunder said it hurled itself into a massive waterfall.

Galsavia's ears twitched rapidly between the noise of the dragons flying above and the water drowning out other sounds. "An army of gremlins could rush at us here, and I would not hear them until we were flattened." He gave Rynan a glance. "Perhaps you should have your sword out in case of an attack?"

Rynan smiled a little as he drew the blade from its sheath. "I think it's likely we shall have *multiple* attacks before we reach the golden crest lair." A few small reptiles similar to two-headed snakes dodged the path before them, and Rynan swiped at a few of the ones that stopped to hiss. The sun beat down on them, and they stopped to take a drink of water from the Siren's shell.

"Thankfully we have safe water to drink. I would be loath to drink from this river." Rynan eyed the dark murky water rushing beside them. Galsavia snorted a laugh and reached back to nip a fly off his flank.

"It is odd that such a barren desert has an endless water supply." The unicorn had fewer qualms about the questionable water and stepped into the edge of the current to cool off. Rynan kept an eye on the bolder dragons that flew lower, showing their daring bravado that melted away when he held his sword out in readiness.

The day wore on, and they came upon a pitiful sight. A baby dragon the size of a small horse had fallen into the river and was clinging to a rock in the center of the foaming water. He was screaming, and there is no sadder sound than a baby dragon in distress. His wings were still too weak to pull him from the water's grip, and his claws were slipping on the mossy rock. His fearful cries rang in their ears, and Rynan didn't hesitate to attempt to rescue him. Shedding his gear and weapons, he made a slip knot with the giant's rope. One end he tied securely to Galsavia's neck; then with the other end of the rope in hand, he dove into the water. He nearly drowned trying to reach the dragonlet. Water filled his ears and mouth, and relentless currents kept dragging him under. Twice he had to pull himself up the rope back toward land, trying to get closer to the distressed animal.

Finally, he grabbed onto the dragon's tail and pulled himself up onto the rock. The little beast screamed louder and swatted at him with a paw. Rynan dodged the weak blow and quickly looped the rope around the long scaly neck. He signaled to Galsavia, who dug his hooves into the dirt and pulled with the strength of an elephant. Rynan hung onto the dragonlet's tail with a vice grip and received several hard kicks in the mouth for his pains, but they made it to shore, wet and bedraggled and Rynan with a bloody lip and nose. The dragon coughed up enough water to drown a host of people, but other than his fright, Rynan felt the little beast was fine.

Before he had quite got his breath back, a massive shadow flew overhead, and a roar that quailed their hearts ripped through the sky. A large dragon, apparently the dragonlet's mother, swept down on them, breathing a torrent of fire. Rynan rolled away, regaining his feet and the sharp sword from the giant in one motion then turned to face her. She hesitated at his fearlessness and glanced at his shining blade for a moment. He wondered at her gaze, but the moment was not long. She rapidly struck at him with her claws aimed at his face. He blocked, ducked, and came up to parry another blow. Back and forth they went, Rynan leaping from her flaming breaths and the dragon dodging slashes from the gleaming blade.

Suddenly the baby dragon gave a little squeak. The mother stopped mid attack and turned back to her child. The baby made squeaks and snuffling sounds as she cuddled it, listening quietly. Slowly she turned back to Rynan. He raised his sword, expecting a refreshed assault. She lowered her head and spoke in a deep wild-sounding voice.

"I fear I just have done you a grave injustice, warrior from foreign realms. My little one says he expected you to slay him as an easy dragon kill, yet instead you saved his life. I cannot thank you enough," and she bowed very low.

Rynan bowed cautiously in return and lowered his weapon. "I have no reason to kill one who has done me no harm," he said respectfully.

She pointed at his sword, "And yet you carry the Dragon Slayer's blade?"

"It was a gift. I know very little of its first owner or former duties."

She seemed unsure for a moment then nodded slowly. "Aye, that would be true, for if you were the great Dragon Slayer, you would be older now."

Rynan was intrigued. "Who was this warrior, for I have never heard his name in any lore or book of tales?"

The dragon glanced around then said quietly "Follow me, and I shall tell you what I know."

With the dragonlet perched on her back, the larger dragon led the way, and Rynan followed with Galsavia. A strange procession they made, walking through the scorched lands—a man and unicorn following a dragon to her lair. Rynan fingered the hilt of the giant's sword and reached back once to see if his own sword was readily available from its sheath on his back. He was not quite sure how this encounter would end and wanted to be ready. When they reached the cave where these dragons dwelled, he tucked the three vials tightly to his belt and marched on, prepared for anything. It was well he was wary, for once inside, a dragon smaller than the mother charged them in a rage. For a few tangled moments, the sword rang, fire raged, and Galsavia's horn struck the hard scales with a shattering clang, but it was mere seconds of this when the young dragon abruptly stopped his attack and stared at Rynan's sword.

"You are the Dragon Slayer. You have returned," it whispered hoarsely.

"Nay, I am not, and I come for one purpose only, and it is not to kill any dragons."

The mother stepped forward then, and everyone sat down in a wide circle around her, keeping their distance from each other. She then began her tale.

"Once, many ages ago, a warrior from an unknown realm came here to retrieve a gem stolen from his people. A dragon had taken it on a raid, and its value was immeasurable. When the warrior tried to retrieve it, a large number of dragons assailed him all at once, but he had a sword that did not melt or break, and he had a massive shield of incredible strength that withstood the teeth of every beast. He beheaded dozens of dragons that day before they finally fled. His armor was not even singed by the flames, and all dragons hid within their caves for moons on end. The warrior retrieved his gem and left our lands, but he warned that he would return if any dared rob his lands again; and as sign of this warning, he left his shield at the top of the volcano, where it stayed for years, and none dared fly beyond the shield's mark.

"But a few decades ago, the dragon of the golden crest said it had been too long and the warrior would not return, and he threw the shield down into the river where it lay for a long time until I retrieved it and hid it here in my hoard, for I thought should the slayer ever return, I might give it back to him as a symbol of peace for me and mine, and when I saw your sword today, I was afraid of you, but thinking you meant harm to my child, I would have fought a hundred dragon slayers to defend my own blood from harm." And she held her head up, with a look in her eye that has cast down warriors in all times—the look of a mother protecting her young.

Rynan stood up and, bowing respectfully, said, "When my journey is complete, I will find out who this warrior was, for in truth, I am rather in awe of his skill. But for now, I am here to do no harm unless harm is meant for me, and I must retrieve a drop of blood from the head of the dragon of the golden crest. My people depend upon it."

All three of the dragons drew back away from him in horror. "Even we," the young dragon gasped. "Even we do not disturb him. He is angered easily and very jealous of his treasure. He will not tolerate the life of anyone inside his lair. You surely attempt suicide!"

"That is quite possible, but I have erred greatly, and it is a deed I must do to repair the wrong I have done."

The young dragon and the baby both looked at the mother. She turned to Rynan and spoke for them all, "We do not wish you ill seeing we are in your debt. Two things we will give you—one is the shield of the Dragon Slayer, for you must be of his blood to be so fearless, and secondly a warning—the dragon of the golden crest has one weakness, as all dragons have, and that is his love of gold, but above all, he knows the power of that drop of blood you seek. No gold can buy it, and no warrior could possibly take it without his permission. You will fail, but at least with the shield and your blade, you may yet survive."

Rynan smiled. "I intend to survive, and I believe I have something of value that he will not refuse if he will let me speak with him."

"If you think there is a possibility of success, then go, and may the fearlessness of a dragon go with you, may your sword be quick, and may your wits be quicker," she answered respectfully, which is a very great compliment from a dragon, for Rynan was the first and perhaps last man that a dragon ever spoke such words to.

Shield in hand, the two friends left for the volcano lair, the end of this journey for them. Again, Rynan thought grimly that he could not fail, for his kingdom was depending on him. He must succeed. "And I will," he whispered, setting his jaw and holding the shield firmly.

They walked through the afternoon, the barren wasteland slowly draping in the shadows of the coming night. Neither spoke as the day wore on, their journey's end weighing too heavily on them for words. The heat of the day made Rynan's breastplate of armor hot to touch, and he warily eyed the inferno leaking from the mountain ahead of them.

They reached the foot of the volcano as the sun was setting. Smoke issued from the mouth of the volcano, and Galsavia mused, "It seems the volcano is ready to spew its lava."

"No, my friend, that is not the volcano. It is the breathing of an angry dragon, and I'll warrant he already knows we're here." They paused for a moment and looked into each other's eyes; each saw the heart of his friend reflecting at him, and they found they had the courage to continue.

They climbed the volcano's steep side and reached the top where large stairs lead down, circling around the mouth, deep into the heart of the heat below, and each wondered if he would be alive to see the sunrise on the morrow.

Part IV

Rynan and Galsavia descended into the depths of the volcano, the heat intensifying with each step. Smoke billowed about, burning their eyes and making it difficult to see. When they finally reached the foot of the stairs, both were gasping for breath, but the burning in Rynan's soul was more than the heat he was enduring. Laying the heavy spear against the stairs, he gained thought about how cumbersome its size was. He glanced about to get his bearings as best he could and saw a high doorway to his left.

"And that is where the dragon will be," he murmured, nodding to Galsavia.

They had to cross a very wide and bare space to reach the doorway, but before they could proceed, a sinister voice spoke out. "How have you dared to come here, trespassers from afar." It echoed over and over in the vast space, and it chilled them to their very souls.

Rynan drew his sword and replied. "We have dared, we are here, and that is all," and both began walking steadily toward the doorway.

A blast of fire shot out from the gaping hole, and both friends dunked behind the shield. Rynan, even in this moment, marveled that the shield was not even warm; it completely refracted the fire and the heat. Both stayed crouched behind the amazing shield and continued forward.

"That was your only warning—there will be no other!" The dragon's voice thundered so that the ground trembled, and another blast, even hotter, shot at them. It was a long time crossing that space to the doorway, being blasted every step and shrieked at. When they finally reached the arch, they were exhausted and nearly deaf from the shattering echoes, but amazingly, they were barely singed except for the end of Galsavia's long mane.

Rynan looked at his friend and smiled. The unicorn smiled back, and that was all. That was a goodbye between dearest of friends—in case this was indeed the end. With that encouragement, they charged into the dragon's den.

Inside it was lit by a dark-red glow from the dragon, the dull light bouncing off the walls and reflecting on the shiny finish of the shield. A long narrow path led to where the dragon sat on an island covered in a mountain of gold. All around the island and on either side of the path, far below, glimmered lava, bubbling and smoldering like the dragon's temper.

"I see you are special indeed, for my flames have no effect on you." Curiosity mingled with fury shone in the scaly beast's bright eyes. His long neck snaked down from his golden nest and reached out as he squinted and stared at his foe. Rynan could make out the golden scales that glittered on the green forehead—the golden crest.

"Your flames do not bother me, and I shall not run from your wrath," Rynan replied stoutly.

The dragon's face slowly stretched into a toothy and malicious grin. "Nay, you shall not run. Once you have come to the lair of the dragon of the golden crest, no one ever leaves…and how convenient that you both have come just when I am so hungry."

The dragon gave a roar that ripped the air about them and dove forward. He came across the path with startling speed, and his snout banged against the shield, for he came too quickly to be more wary of the prey. He coiled back and stared blankly at Rynan. All others—armor and all—had easily been swallowed. Why was this one so different? The dragon looked Rynan over carefully. His eyes strayed to the sword then again looked back to the shield that Rynan held before him. The truth dawned, and the dragon withdrew abruptly to his island.

"I was sure you were dead, Dragon Slayer. You have come back to destroy me and take all my treasure." It growled, and its claws grasped pawfuls of gold, clutching it greedily.

"I do not want even one coin or jewel from you," Rynan replied, deciding not to broach the subject of the Dragon Slayer's person.

"Oh?" the dragon asked suspiciously. "Then what do you wish?"

"Something of greater value," Rynan answered. It was becoming apparent that the dragon was not only selfish and vain, but also a great coward, never leaving his lair to fight unless he knew he faced a weaker opponent—a brute among the dragon kind—that's why they feared him so. The dragon glanced at the sword again, and by the cunning look on its face, Rynan knew that the dragon was calculating the chances against the power of that sword.

"So, you want a drop of blood, eh?" the dragon said slowly, his claws playing with a ruby of enormous dimensions. "Even the Dragon Slayer cannot get that which he wishes, for the power of it is useless if you slay me, and I'll never willingly give it." The great beast turned and locked his eyes with Rynan's, for in truth, the dragon was quite safe now. Rynan knew he could not slay him—the old lore was quite specific on that detail—and he also knew he could not leave without that drop of blood.

"I will buy it" was the warrior's response.

A loud and unpleasant laugh echoed in the cavern.

"What could you possibly have of worth that could equal such thing?"

"A mermaid tear of the purest form."

The laugh ceased instantly, and the dragon gave a long hard look at the warrior.

"A mermaid tear? Worth the ransom of a hundred kings?"

"Worth more even, for it is a tear from the Siren."

And the dragon could not help his jaw dropping in shock then, "You have seen the Siren and lived? And taken a tear too? Your powers are beyond belief. Perhaps you are too strong," and here his face grew darkly suspicious. "How has one so young succeeded in so great a thing?"

"I have succeeded in many things and sadly failed at other things" was the honest response. "But where I succeed, I have always done so with the help of a friend and a firmness of purpose."

The dragon was silent for a moment then slowly spoke. "I do not see any magic or power in your ways. I do not believe you can succeed in this mission." His voice had become softer, more trancelike.

"Perhaps, but I will not let my light fade just so someone else's shadow won't feel threatened." Rynan gripped his sword hilt until his hand ached with the strain. He would not let the dragon's silken tone numb him as had happened to other dragon-fighting knights. Rynan was too familiar with history to allow it to repeat in him again. It was better to be a lightning strike than a thunder roll, merely echoing the power of the flash.

There was a moment of stillness in the cavern, then in an instant, the dragon was upon him. This was by far the worst they had endured on the journey, for the shield protected them well, but still the dragon's teeth or claws clipped them here and there, and the flames were unbearable. It seemed a long time that they fought in the light of that dull red glow. It was too late when Rynan realized the dragon was slowly working them across to the narrow path, only a few feet wide and very long with the boiling lava on each side. The clever beast was cutting off their retreat and steadily forcing them toward the looming nest.

The dragon swooped down over them, and Rynan raised his shield; but a claw from the dragon snagged Galsavia, and with a shriek, the unicorn slipped off the ledge. For a moment he dangled, his front hooves losing traction as his body slid further down. The dragon roared a laugh and flew a wide circle, coming back to devour the beast. Those short seconds were all Rynan needed. He grabbed the vial with the mermaid tear, opened it, and poured the tear into the lava below them. Then he flung himself toward the dragon who was gliding in, mouth open toward Galsavia.

That same moment the tear dropped to the lava below, Galsavia fell, and Rynan's blade stabbed true into the dragon's forehead. The dragon let out a horrid scream and shot up to the cavern ceiling.

As Galsavia fell into the fire below, the tear touched the surface, and the lava vanished, cool clear water flowing in place of the liquid heat. The magic of the Siren's tear was more powerful than the anger of the dragon. Galsavia crashed with a splash into the beautiful blue of the mermaid tear—a clear, surreal light rippling all around the cavern.

Rynan slid down the edge of the path and with his third vial carefully scraped the drop of dark-red blood into it, locking it for safekeeping. Then the dragon blasted his fire at Rynan in a fury that would have terrified anyone, but Rynan stood and laughed mockingly. The many hours of reading had also mentioned this. Now that he possessed that drop of blood, the dragon could not harm him, for it gave the warrior dragon power, making him impervious to heat. The dragon, in panic, retreated to his nest and snarled fearfully.

Rynan strolled toward him, sword pointed. "Now you will obey me, great lizard. Come!"

And the dragon knew he must. He slithered down and laid his head at Rynan's feet. "Slay me now, for you are surely the great Dragon Slayer of old."

"I do not wish to slay you. I have what I came for, and now I will add a command. First, you will rescue my friend."

The dragon promptly obeyed and carefully picked up the unicorn, flying him back up to the path and gently setting him down by Rynan. Galsavia was none the worse for the wetting and was highly amused and relieved at the change in the dragon.

"What further orders have you, master?" the dragon asked respectfully.

"I wish you to bring me a drop from the Siren's water below, one drop to refill my vial."

The dragon did as he was bid and returned with the glittering vial renewed with its contents.

"Well done. Now I wish you to fly me back to my lands. Then you will be free to return to your lair. I will not take your life as you fear, but I may require your services in the future, and you must return to me if I call."

The dragon bowed. "I am grateful."

Galsavia and Rynan climbed onto the broad back, and the dragon flew to his nest, snatching up the giant ruby, and away they flew to the top of the volcano. Rynan wondered at the dragon adding the weight of the ruby to his load but decided it was not to be concerned with. His singing burns were bothering him more than he liked to acknowledge, and he was too grateful that the dragon was willing to carry them back to start an argument.

Outside in the open air, it was early morning. A beautiful waterfall now flowed down to a ravine where once lava had dripped. Already green things were beginning to grow in the place of the scorched lands.

The flight was the best part of their long journey. Rynan was jubilant to return home successful, and now all his thoughts could be turned to rescuing the wolf and restoring the magic bane.

They flew rapidly for many days, only stopping when Rynan deemed the dragon needed to rest. The beast would not take one break without permission, and Rynan was kind enough to notice when their mount was tired.

Each portal was passed through quickly. The dragon, being a magical being, had no need of artifacts to access the power and with a roar could open each gateway. There was one day on the flight where far below they saw the serpent's lair, the giant's castle, and other familiar sights slip behind them to the horizon. Then came a day when they entered the Siren's realm and a flood of memories washed over Rynan. The pool was still rippling and the seagulls still crying in the distance. It made Rynan remember his failure more clearly to be this close to home. He thought of Galsavia's words and tried to see himself in that light, but he found he was not successful in it. The day at last came when they could see the final portal's flow in the distance—the gate back into the Forest Kingdom. They were nearly home.

Rynan felt that the dragon had more than fairly served them and ordered the beast to land in front of the portal. The dragon alighted with a great stirring of wind, and they dismounted. Once they had alighted, the dragon turned to them and bowed. In his front claws he still held the giant ruby. Lowering his head to the ground, he offered it out to them. "That is thanks for my life."

Rynan bowed back and accepted it reverently, for never in recorded history had a dragon given a gift, and perhaps it may never be repeated again in time as we know it.

Rynan remembered their bargain and spoke. "If I need you again, I will call."

"And I will come," the dragon said in a tone that spoke as a friend and ally, and they parted ways.

Rynan turned to his friend. "Ready to return?"

The unicorn nodded, and the two marched toward the portal. Rynan could hardly believe they had succeeded. They had survived the journey and returned with the protection needed to keep his kingdom safe. He looked over at his friend, and Galsavia responded with a kind smile. "I never once doubted you could do it."

Rynan smiled back, his throat tight with emotion. What had he ever done to deserve such a friend? He struck the ground with the spear, hoping it was for the last time, and the gate shivered into view. Galsavia stopped him before they entered. "I think you should ride as we enter. Your burns are still healing, and it will solidify to the kingdom that we are a team."

Rynan argued as he had no wish to show his friend at such a level of servitude in their kingdom, but Galsavia would not allow a debate. Eventually, for the sake of returning as quickly as possible, a very humble guardian swung up onto the unicorn's back. He strapped the spear awkwardly to his back, and they stepped into the hazy circle.

The dark night was illuminated by a pale moon as they emerged back into their own realm, and they both realized something was wrong as the city gates came into view.

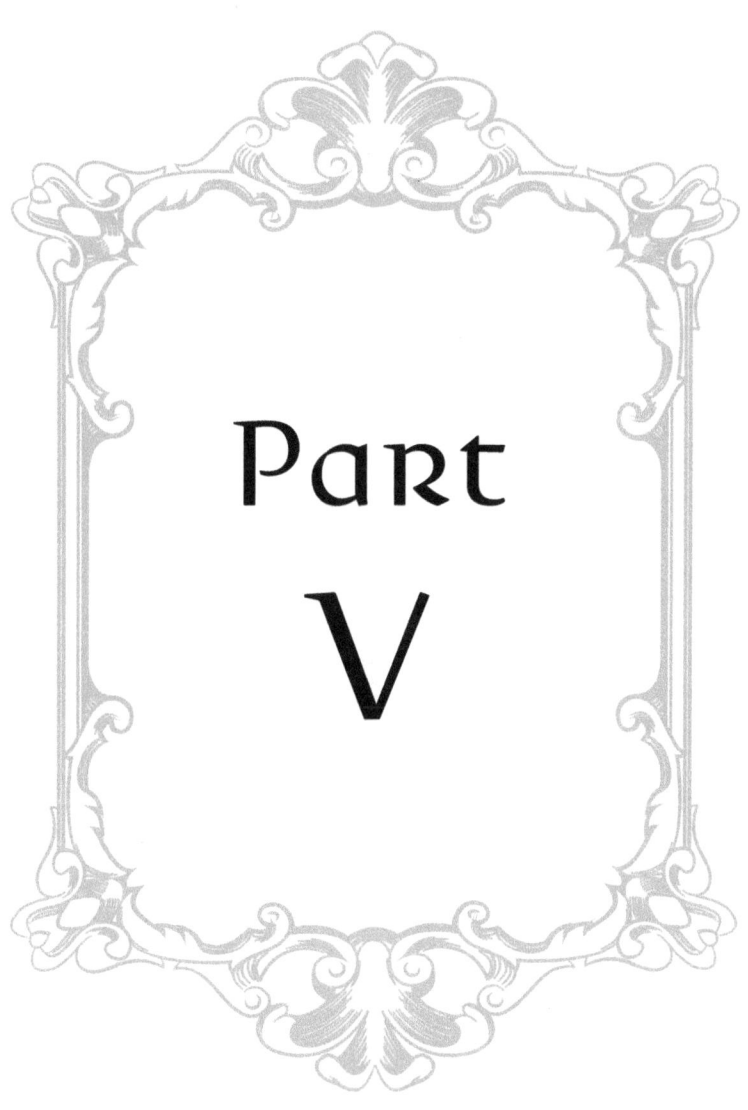

Part V

Rynan and Galsavia entered the gates and wondered that no guard questioned them. No archers stood upon the ramparts, and no lookout hailed them from the towers. The kingdom was dreadfully silent. Rynan's fears mounted as they continued. Everywhere there were signs of a fight and no signs of life. Signs of fierce fires marred the walls and buildings. Something dreadful had happened here.

Finally, Galsavia began galloping to the castle in the center of the city. If the people were in hiding, that is where they would be, for the castle walls were thick and high, and a stream flowed through its center.

Reaching the castle, the unicorn jolted to an abrupt stop. There was blood—old and dry, caked—upon the steps and on the locked gate. Were they too late? Had the gremlins attacked and won the kingdom?

Rynan leapt off his friend's back and raced up the steps, pounding his fist upon the gate. "It's all my fault!" he gasped. "There must be someone left…there has to be!" He banged on the iron gate and yelled, and Galsavia kicked his hooves upon the metal. At long last, far within the castle, they heard a voice.

"Come and slay us if you must, but do it quickly."

The voice was weak and faint, and Rynan quickly called back. "It is friends that come, not foes. I am Rynan, once guardian of the magic bane, and Galsavia, the unicorn in the king's service."

"There is no king left here," the voice replied mournfully. "But I shall let you in. Be you friend or foe, it matters not."

The gate was slow to yield but at last is groaned open, and there stood a small huddled group of fearful villagers. They were so sorrowful and pathetic that Rynan was aghast for a moment. "You were gone long, warrior…seven long months…and you have returned to find us no longer a kingdom, merely the shadow of the past." And the speaker began weeping profusely so that all the people sobbed. It was some time before Rynan calmed the group down.

"Please tell me what happened to the king?"

The speaker, a frail little woman, who looked as if she had lost her life along with her courage, shook her head. "The gremlins came when you left. They must have had a spy tell them that our warrior was gone. We fought them successfully at first, then they had the great vultures of the West come. They came as a united army, flying about on the backs of their birds, and we could not withstand the onslaught. The king was captured. They took him away—we do not know where. Those that are left pay tribute to the gremlins by leaving food or clothing in the courtyard, but we never show our faces for fear of the vultures."

Rynan was silent for a moment, and his heart was greatly grieved. "All of this is my doing, but I will correct it as best as I may. Are there any young people left?"

The old women slowly nodded. "Yes, there are some young ones left, but"—she hesitated—"we keep them locked up, for they are the last of our children, and we cannot bear to lose them."

"Take me to them," the warrior replied softly.

It was a sad group that huddled about the warrior and the unicorn as they made their way to the great hall. The door was boarded up and chained, and from the inside the young ones were called out to be released so they might fight.

The crowd hesitated to open the door. "Please, warrior, they are all we have left."

"Open the door, else all you will ever have are wasted memories. For victory can only come with unity." Rynan's tone was very stern, and the people hastened to obey. The door was flung back, and twelve sturdy young men and women came out, blinking in the sunlight and glaring at their captors.

"Any who wish to be free of the gremlins and restore the kingdom, follow me," Rynan said, turning on heel and walking toward the center courtyard.

All twelve followed eagerly with the crowd trailing behind hesitantly. Weapons lay scattered about, mostly rusted; and as he walked, Rynan gathered them up. He leaned the portal spear against a stone wall as he filled his arms with weapons. The warriors mimicked his movement, collecting weapons, and the courtyard was soon more orderly in appearance. Above them, shadows of vultures glided about, and Rynan handed out weapons as he walked toward the central gate. His goal was to get into the armory and properly arm his new soldiers with shields and the swords cleaned from rust, but still a rusty blade may be a service as Rynan soon proved.

A bold vulture swooped low over Rynan, screeching, claws extended, for the beast smelled that here was a leader and he must be eliminated. Rynan's training had him react without hesitation. He swung a long rusted blade at the claws and, grabbing the injured foot of the bird, dragged him to the ground. Quicker than a blink, he pulled his knife and stabbed the creature of filth before it had time to scream. Overhead the other vultures flew, shrieking away to warn the gremlins that a warrior had come.

"Quickly, to the armory, all of you!" Rynan shouted, and everyone ran swiftly, for Rynan's small victory had put the heart back into the people.

Once inside, they secured the door and set about briskly, readying themselves. The older folk gathered the last of the food and rationed out enough for a few days, but it was meager portions, and Rynan set his mind to have the victory in two days before anyone need go hungry.

He ate only a bite and gave his food away to the elderly, for his journey had made him strong and hardy, and he had often been used to having little to eat.

For hours they worked nonstop, training, practicing, and preparing weapons; but later on the first evening, Rynan had gone to the tower at the top of the armory and released the last of the kingdom messenger birds. One, a seagull, he sent to the sea realm to call aid from Thalassa and her people. The second bird was a wren, and he sent it to land of the giants, straight to Jahonbran's castle. The last was a swallow, and his orders were carried to the dragon of the golden crest. All the birds carried the same message: *Come as soon as you may. I have need of you.* He had simply signed it *Rynan*.

The birds were magic trained, and each wore a small gold band with a tiny portal stone attached. They would be able to fly to their destinations with ease, but would they receive the reply he so desperately needed?

Rynan worked hard along with the rest of the small band as they prepared, but all the while, his heart followed the trails of the birds, and his lips sometimes whispered, "Please come, for I have need of you."

The next few days, Rynan found that this small group of fighters possessed a determination and stamina that made him proud. They learned everything he taught them and had a fearlessness that encouraged his heart. Several of the middle-aged survivors had started training as well, and with the added numbers, cheer rose among them. The older folk even took heart and helped clean and ready armor.

Rynan wasn't sure how long the charred walls would hold off an attack, but he had no doubt an attack was coming. His thoughts were often on the wolf and the king, hoping against hope that they both still lived, and he schemed and plotted how a rescue could be possible. His greatest chance lay in if his allies answered his call for help. He did not believe that they wouldn't show so much as he feared they would not arrive in time, before it was too late—before *he* was too late. He had failed so miserably, allowing his kingdom to be put in this plight, but his journey had been successful. Surely he could prove to himself that he could correct his mistakes. The flickering portal spear often reminded him that it was true, he had retrieved the required element. He often checked on the room that held the vial containing the dragon blood mostly to reassure himself it wasn't a dream. The drop of dragon's blood was safe. If he could only ensure it stayed that way.

Part VI

Rynan never once showed doubt or fear he felt as he prepared his small troop for battle. They needed to believe in themselves; Rynan had to show how much he believed they could fight so they could see it too—and he did believe in them. They were determined and drilled with a desperate sort of faith, but long before they were ready for battle, the gremlins came, pounding upon the gates, burning walls and working closer to the indestructible armory.

At last, they could wait no more. A siege was not something they were equipped to handle. Rynan knew that they were as ready as the time could make them.

He spent the last evening checking the armor and weapons and encouraging everyone. They knew they were going to battle, and he was encouraged in their determination. Their faces reflected in the torchlight, grim and ready, but they were young. Rynan grieved, knowing some of them might not be around to see tomorrow evening.

Arming everyone with the weapons they had salvaged, he called them to attention. "We go out united with a common purpose. We will not let those left here to perish. We will leave such a memory on our attackers as to cause fear in their hearts for a thousand years to come. If we lose this battle, it will not be of cowardice. You already rank among the greats of history. If we are not here when the sun sets, let us show the gremlins that the warriors of the Forest Kingdom know how to die."

That was all. The group set their helmets firmly on their heads and drew their swords. Rynan had been asked by his little army to wear the helmet with the iron unicorn horn, the helm that showed the wearer was a commander. Rynan had agreed. If it gave them more hope, he would do anything for them.

Galsavia tossed his horn and snorted, his body tense and battle ready beside his friend. The door was thrown open, and the battle began. The gremlins were taken aback, for they had not expected to encounter warriors and had not been aware that any were left that could wield a sword. Rynan charged in the lead, brandishing the Dragon Slayer sword in one hand and his father's blade in the other. The Dragon Slayer's blade seemed to glow and was a flaming blur of death to the gremlins, who fell before him in masses until the rest fled, howling and reassembling down by the gates. They would find their courage before long and attack anew, and Rynan, glancing about at his soldiers that stood, bloody but undaunted, knew that here were warriors truly such as the land had never seen.

Soon the enemy came charging back with a flock of ghastly vultures and a few mangy wild dogs added to their ranks. Again, they defeated the onslaught, and again they were attacked. In his mind, Rynan knew too well this was the end, for they were only seven fighters left now, the others having fallen. Rynan saw a group of attackers break off as they headed to the interior of the building, their grotesques noses twitching. They had scented the dragon blood. They would destroy it. He lunged at them, fury making him strong in his attacks. Galsavia soon joined him, and together they defended the entryway. It seemed a very long time that they held that doorway. The enemy seemed to never slack in numbers, and his arms were growing weary with the weight of his weapons. Looking out over the fighting, he saw that his troops were wearing down. It had been a long fight, and their enemy showed renewed aggression at their loss of numbers. It even rather seemed that the enemy was multiplying.

With a last desperate effort, he shouted, "Let them quiver at the sound of you!"

The soldiers yelled madly, Galsavia snorted and reared, and blood flowed even more as they cast themselves deeper and deeper into the enemies' numbers; and just as Rynan felt hope, he looked up and saw hundreds of gremlins racing down into the city from hillsides beyond the city.

"We are finished," he whispered even as he kept on fighting. He turned with savage rage on his next opponent, fury boiling that his group of brave fighters would be taken down.

But what was that sound? A roar of rage too loud, too deep for a man rang out deafeningly, and a surge of giants charged from the north, destroying the armies in their way. Hope blossomed in the soul of the guardian. The gremlin numbers were still overwhelming, but help had come. They fought on, but even with aid, the fury of the battle did not wane.

As the afternoon sun came down, hot and fierce, a shadow drifted over. Looking up, Rynan saw the dragon of the golden crest flanked by dozens of smaller dragons. They swooped into the battle, shooting red flames out before them. The dragons had answered the call for help too. The cheer that rose from his band were feeble from weariness, but still they fought on, and still the gremlins came.

Rynan's arms shook with the strain of battle. The heat was intense, and his hands burned from the hot sword's metal. Suddenly a breeze stirred, and a spray of mist coated the air. Could it be? With a renewed energy, Rynan vaulted himself onto the shoulder of the gremlin he was currently fighting. He pivoted in air, grabbing the dilapidated castle wall, clinging to where the mortar had fallen out. He scrambled to the top of the wall and looked out at the massive river that flowed against the castle wall. A wave nearly as tall as the towers rose up before him then was abruptly thrown back as scores of merfolk stepped out of the water. Their tails shimmered with magic and turned to legs as they surged into battle. Thalassa had come. The merfolk numbers were vast, and the weapons they carried were strange and deadly looking. All of his allies had kept their word and come to his aid. He was amazed and humbled.

The gremlins saw the three great armies bearing down on them and turned to run through the gate, but Rynan had rallied his troops, and they barred the way. The gremlins, seeing Rynan, a unicorn, and the warriors with blood dripping from their blades, broke rank, screaming and shouting as they ran wherever they could. The giants, dragons, and merfolk gave no mercy in their pursuit of the enemy.

It was soon over and only one hostage left, begging, who was dragged before Rynan.

"Oh, spare me," it squeaked and writhed.

"I have no reason to, but I wish to go to the Mount of the Dark Moon, and you will take me there."

At this, the creature screamed, "Kill me now, for we dare not go down now that I have failed. My master is there in the center of the mountain. He is very cruel and wicked. I dare not take his enemy to him!"

"You *will*," Rynan thundered, and the gremlin deferred.

They had to wait until the next day to leave. Guard rotations needed to be assigned, and generals met with Rynan to determine how to work the three armies together while the leaders were away, and the dead had to be buried.

The afternoon was somber, as many warriors were laid to rest, and there were not a few tears shed. Rynan was grateful to those that had been willing to follow his orders and give the ultimate sacrifice. There was a great deal of guilt added to his burdens as well. He was almost past the point of tears. He felt more numb and wretched than ever before. Galsavia was standing beside him as he gave the eulogies. When he was finished and the crowd dispersed, the unicorn stepped in front of him.

"Rynan, it is time to let some things go."

"I just buried them. They died because of me…because I lost the magic bane. It's my fault."

"They died warriors, and they were proud to serve under you. Don't take that honor away from them."

Rynan swallowed hard and finally looked into the unicorn's knowing eyes. "I mourn their loss. I owe them that."

"Yes, they deserve to be missed and have earned the right to be praised, but they wanted to fight with you. They forgave you a long time ago for the loss of the magic bane, or they would never have followed you. You need to forgive yourself—they would want you to—and if you owe them anything, it is not guilt but honor. Don't disparage their pride in you. It does them no credit."

Rynan took several minutes to calm his inner turmoil. Finally, he spoke. "I may never be able to forgive myself, but for their sake, I will try."

Galsavia nodded, hearing more in his voice than the words. Together they rejoined the armies and began preparations to leave the next morning.

After thanks and praises to their alliances, Rynan, Galsavia, Jahonbran, the dragon of the golden crest, and Thalassa all proceeded toward the Mount of the Dark Moon. Each of the allies had left warriors behind, charging them to protect the city until they returned. A general from each army was chosen to oversee the kingdoms safety while they were away. A coalition was formed, and the remaining castle residents were left in capable hands. Special guard instructions were given for protecting the drop of dragon blood from any spies that might come lurking back.

With his mind at ease for his people, Rynan once again took up the portal spear. The five warriors walked together and went through the castle gate. Rynan used perhaps more force than necessary as he stabbed the ground, for the gateway opened with a loud crack and was far larger than usual. The others could have lent their magic for portal travel, but allowing Rynan to command the gateway showed that they considered him the leader on this mission. He was grateful for their confidence in him—it gave him courage to have these beings of power willing to have his back when facing the darkest power the world knew. The gremlin that would guide them through the fortress hung limply from the dragon's claws. His occasional squeals and curses were ignored as the door shimmered before them. All of them marched through swiftly; they were heading in for war. Rynan slung the portal spear into the strap he had made the evening before to carry the large magic weapon and keep it from hindering him in the coming fight.

The land belonging to the dark fortress was ghastly to behold, full of slime and a dark smoky sky above. They traveled rapidly, for going in secret was not possible. With the surrounding land barren, all ways to approach the Mount of the Dark Moon were visible. Deserts were crossed, crags were scaled, and Rynan felt neither heat nor tiredness. They hoped only to be swift enough to stop any counter plans.

They were soon standing at a great stone gate, which led into a massive yawning hole, spewing shadows as if darkness itself dwelled within the Mount of the Dark Moon. The gremlin groveled at the entry, begging release, which Rynan did not heed.

"Take us to the wolf," he ordered. Turning to the dragon, he asked, "Would you light our way?" and with a soft breath, the dragon blew a red-and-gold flame out of his nostrils, keeping it lit as they walked down into the blackness. Thalassa's hair flickered in the light, sending a surreal blue glow about the cavern. Their steps echoed with the click of Rynan's boots, the clop of Galsavia's hooves, the thud of the giant, the soft muted scratching of the dragon, and the almost noiseless tread of the merlady. For some time, they walked, turning into passages leading to other passages and always, always leading down. Once a ghastly hoard of bats flew into their faces, but Rynan knocked them aside without halting stride. Soon they came to a massive room where grotesque things hung about.

The gremlin smiled coolly. "This is our kitchen. We keep no prisoners, only pantries."

The group stopped for the first time since their descent. So the wolf bane was dead and the king also, along with his knights.

Part VII

The grating laugh of gremlin echoed viciously about them all for a moment until Galsavia pressed his horn into the creature's throat. The others nodded their approval and waited to see what the warrior would decide.

Rynan was struck numb, looking about in horror, then his face changed darkly. This was a deception, just like the lute player, a front to hide the truth. He grabbed the gremlin by the throat and held him up. "You lie, scum. Your master has dungeons with prisoners *alive* in them. They are alive, suffering torture somewhere in this hole, and you *will* take us to them."

He dropped the creature, who rapidly led them on until they came to a massive door with iron bolts and heavy lead braces.

"In there," the gremlin whispered. "The master lives in there. I have never seen beyond this door, and you shall never see the outside world again, for you cannot fool him. He knows you're here," and the beast smiled wickedly despite his evident fear.

Rynan turned to the giant. "Open the door."

With a nod, the giant smashed his club into the massive structure. Once, twice, three times he thundered against it before it shattered to the ground. Darkness reeked out of the doorway as the group stood around, staring into the hollow room. The darkness seemed to move, and a cloaked figure stepped through the doorway. A hood hid his face so that only his eyes, glowing like red coals, showed in the shadows.

The gremlin screamed and would have run away, but the dragon caught him by a claw and detained him.

The cloaked figure spoke in a silky, dark voice. "Ah, so you have come, guardian of the magic bane...or shall I say the curse to the kingdom. For you have led them to ruin, and I have achieved my end."

The truth dawned upon Rynan, and the figure laughed.

"Yes, it was I who lured you from you post with a magic lyre and I who had the young wolf stolen. I knew you would go for the drop of the great dragon's blood and would go to the Siren for vials and to the giant who might bestow a gift and help unlock the treasures of the serpent's cave, and who else could gain the shield of the Dragon Slayer but one such as you? And I have waited long for you to be ready to win these for me. You are the greatest of the guardians and yet you fell easiest, for those who are gifted the most are also most easy to tempt. You didn't even want to be a guardian, but you were born one, and the role is yours no matter how you wish it weren't," and here the being laughed long and eerily. Rynan felt a wave a sickness come over him.

Galsavia is pressed against his shoulder and said quietly, "One may fail and yet redeem themselves."

Rynan looked over at his friend, feeling something awaken in him—something he had never understood before—but the faithfulness of his friend was making it become clear. Slowly he turned to the master of evil. "Yes, I failed. Yes, I brought about much ruin, and I am grieved of myself, but these weapons and gifts I have earned were for my people and to save the magic bane. I cannot undo the past, but I can rescue the future...and you are right, the pressure of being a guardian is exhausting. I've often wished it had not fallen to me. I've often wished my lot had been a different calling, but a guardian is my birthright, my role. I was born to it, and until I die, it is mine to uphold with every ounce of my being.

"We cannot choose what gifts or places we are born to, but we can determine how to use what is given to us, and while your gremlins did succeed in their attacks, still it did not bring about the demise of the world. We are few, but we are strong. Having reliable allies is a powerful thing, as you see by those who stand with me, and those who have friends are rich in ways that cannot be measured. You, sorcerer, have neither allies nor friends, and you will never possess either. Darkness has minions and armies, but it can never have the privilege of holding the trust of another. So here in your hole, in the bowels of the Mount of the Dark Moon, prepare to perish—alone."

With a shriek of rage, the cloaked being unleashed a power that thundered until the ground shook and everyone fell back with the blast. Rynan drew his sword and braced himself for the attack. Dark magic, overwhelming and poisonous, filled the cave. The friends all braced as it enveloped them, causing searing pain.

Galsavia's breath came out in sharp gasps. "My friends," he whinnied. "Each must use their own power but as a team to defeat an enemy of this strength."

The sorcerer snarled and threw a shower of bolts at the unicorn, but Rynan leapt in front of his friend, shielding them both with his shield. Further enraged now, the sorcerer plunged toward Rynan, but the dragon stepped forward and breathed a blast of fire so hot that the sorcerer's cape leapt into blue flames. The sorcerer screamed and turned toward the dragon, but the giant swung his club and knocked their enemy to the wall. Undaunted, the sorcerer stood and came running back, but Thalassa (who had traveled with wisps of water from the sea wrapping about her) raised her hands and let the water grow until it engulfed him. He screamed and shouted in rage as he drowned in the never-ending whirlpool, and just as he came flailing out of water, Galsavia pinned him to the ground.

The dark one shuddered then laughed. "I don't die so easily," and he gathered his magic to himself, sending another burst of force out, knocking them back again. Rynan poised his sword and marched forward.

"You can't kill me. That sword you hold is too powerful for you. It was held by one far stronger than you will ever be. You are a failure and nothing like the great slayer of old," the sorcerer said, laughing while his eyes glowed red and hateful.

"Before my journey through the realms, I could not have killed you, but with what I know now and with the power in this sword from the Dragon Slayer, I can. This sword cannot be broken, cannot be dulled, and cannot be stopped…and I *can* wield it." Then he ran the blade through the black cloak, for the sorcerer with all his dark magic could not withstand the power of that two-edged blade.

There was something akin to an earthquake, and the sorcerer's cloak swirled, melting as the sorcerer screamed, "Another lifetime I'll be back, and someone else will fall. I'll be back. I'm not done yet…" The voice faded as the cloak and the person simply melted into thin air.

The dragon of the golden crest puffed out a spark. "He will be back…maybe not here…but he will reappear someday in another shape to mar the world again with his evil deeds."

Rynan nodded. "I will write all these things down and pass the sword on to the next generation that they may have the wisdom and the weapon to withstand him."

As they spoke, the darkness began to fold down on itself like the smoke from a dying fire until the entire mount was simply a large rock and they all stood in the glorious sunshine. The gremlin, the blackness, the dead things of evil were all gone, and there just ahead of them sat the wolf pup, the magic bane, his cage having vanished with its dark master. He blinked solemnly in the brightness then howled once upon recognizing Rynan, his guardian. Rynan picked him up, hugging him despite the rules to maintain respect for the magic banes. Hugging was probably not allowed, but at the moment, he couldn't find it in himself to care. He turned to see many freed prisoners and as well as his own king walking toward him. All the prisoners bore wounds and scars from their time in the dungeons, but they were free now. It seemed to take several minutes for that to register with them. They had hoped in vain for so long. When at last they did realize the truth, the moment was overwhelming. Some wept, and many clung to one another in desperate hugs, eyes squinting from the sunlight. Dirt and blood smudged their faces, but it could not dampen their joy. Their minds had caught up with the moment, and they *knew* they were free.

The king stopped before Rynan, his bearing still powerful despite his time chained in the dank cell. Rynan bowed as his king approached, still clinging desperately to the wolf pup. It was surprisingly Galsavia that came forward and told the king what had transpired, how the kingdom had been saved by Rynan and his allies. The king then turned to the very quiet and abashed warrior.

"Guardian, you can see that your error caused great harm, and yet you are the most powerful guardian to have lived, for you have ended the dark rule, erased the gremlins, found friends, and returned with wisdom beyond your years. We all thank you," and the king pulled him to his feet to embrace him.

Rynan shook his head and pulled back, his head hanging. "They suffered because of me. I do not deserve your thanks, my liege."

The king gave him an understanding smile. "It was a hard time for all of us, and you suffered as we did, even more so as guilt has haunted you…but, Rynan, do you know why we truly lost our kingdom while you were away?"

"Because I was not there to defend you all as guardian with the bane. I failed in my duty."

"No, warrior, that is not why we fell. The kingdom lost hope. The army lost courage. They did not have the strength to fight on. They depended—perhaps too much—on the protection of the magic bane and forgot they were warriors trained to defend and protect to their last breath. I fought the gremlins until the world ran dark with blood, and the remaining soldiers fled in despair. I was captured, and I confess in that dark void of a cell my hope wavered as well.

"But then you came back, guardian of the magic bane. You rallied the few citizens left and reminded them to have *faith*, and that is why you succeeded. You lost belief in yourself but never lost it for your people. You believed they could win, and you held onto that thought so surely that they learned to believe it as well. Despite your earlier failure, you embraced the hope of success for the sake of those you care about. That is the essence of faith: when all hope seems lost, to see the light when it cannot be seen."

Rynan felt his throat go tight, and this time, when the king wrapped his arms about him, he had the courage to face the hug; and in that moment, he finally found he had the courage to forgive himself.

The group rested for a day before beginning the journey back to the Forest Kingdom, their new allies keeping them company the entire way home. Rynan was overwhelmed at the support and respect the mermaid, giant, and dragon continued to show him as if he was their leader—an honor he did not feel his deserved but they gave without reservation. As always, Galsavia was by his side, not even remotely surprised that Rynan had earned such respect from others.

"You are worthy of your title, guardian, more now than ever before," the unicorn stated quietly in his friend's ear. Rynan marveled at the faithfulness of his dearest friend. In his heart he felt a fierce love rise up to always defend him and serve the kingdom they called home.

It was a joyous party that crossed back into the Forest Kingdom, and it was with great celebration that the survivors welcomed the victors back, and in all lands, there was rejoicing, for many knew that the tempter of their time had been defeated; and so long as Rynan held the blade, they were safe. There was a new understanding of what the magic bane meant as well. It was there to protect them, yes, but it was the courage of the guardian that keep the wolf safe enough to use the magic, and they now realized they could fight a foe even without the aid of the stars. It awakened a new strength to their souls and a light in their eyes. They were not helpless humans—they were warriors—and they realized all of them were in some form a guardian and that the protection of the magic bane should not all fall on one person's shoulders.

The magic wolf bane was restored to his place, howling with delight at being home. At his presence, the drop of dragon's blood suddenly burst into a star jewel, brighter than a million diamonds. It lit the entire known world with its light, chasing away darkness and ignorance and fear, for a long-forgotten prophesy had spoken that when a magic wolf and a drop of dragon's blood both graced the hall at the same moment, the beginning of the great ends would start—a time of peace and healing for all lands and all peoples.

Rynan's seven warriors were given portions as heads of state and came to be great leaders and wise counselors in the land.

The king had Rynan's position elevated so that all who could assist in protecting the wolf would do so. Rynan found himself as head of a small army, all eager to train as guardians. They zealously assisted in his work—from the tiniest details to the hardest tasks—aiding with protection, patrols, food supplies, and caretaking. No job was too menial, and all respected their leader with fierce passion.

Rynan found he had the leisure now to read the old writings to his heart's content and searched far and wide for information on the Dragon Slayer. He even went to other kingdoms, looking to know the whereabouts of the great warrior, but that person was not to be found. Rynan's allies assisted willingly in his search, all earnest in the hope of discovery until at last they concluded, as Galsavia said, "Perhaps it's not so much the man himself but his convictions and skills of weaponry that really matter, and now there is a new generation that has profited from his works and a new bearer of his sword to guard the world as he did."

And so, though he searched for most of his life, Rynan finally ended the endeavor with having the entire account of all he knew of the Dragon Slayer recorded in the scrolls of history.

And here the tale concludes, Rynan and Galsavia remained close friends for all their days. All their allies made alliances with one another that are still unbroken to this day. They often gathered their peoples together for feasting and the pleasure of one another's company, but Rynan's influence went deeper than this and was long reflected in the hearts of his friends. Sometimes out upon the sea a kindly wave brings sea-weary sailors home; this is a wave of Thalassa, whose heart is full of kindness now that Rynan had set her free, and poor places in the world sometimes find themselves a store of unexpected and much-needed wealth; that is from the giant Jahonbran, for he has learned generosity from Rynan; and sometimes a terrible storm arises in the night: this is the dragon of the golden crest fighting the dark creatures of the night winds, striving to keep the world as safe as he can, for he has learned bravery from Rynan. All of these good things came about, for though many must pay the consequences of one person's failure, yet many can have the blessings of that person's redemption; but they must pick up the sword and fight the sin that so easily besets them and run their race in life, for no one can run it for them.

And this tale of wisdom was recorded by Rynan, who told it to another, and they continued to pass it on until it came to me, and now it has passed on to you. May you use the lessons well.

THE END

Truth becomes legend,
Legend becomes myth,
Myth becomes fantasy.
And yet,
There always the grain of truth
And lesson to be learned in the tale.

Written by Rynan, Guardian of the Magic Bane,
from his personal records at the end of his years.

All Biblical references from the KJV edition.

ACKNOWLEDGMENTS

Many thanks to The Ewings team.
Your dedication to my writing is a blessing.

www.ingramcontent.com/pod-product-compliance
Lightning Source LLC
LaVergne TN
LVHW041713060526
838201LV00043B/709